To my Zen Masters, Kai and Riven.
With love and a great big YES, Mia.

This book is given with love
To:

From:

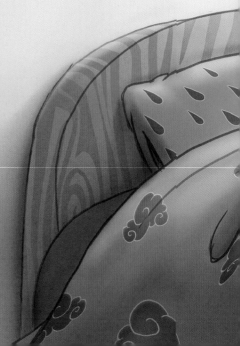

YES DAYS
NO DAYS

Written by:
Mia Von Scha

Illustrated by:
Mirna Stevanovic

I bounce out of bed
in the morning and I say,

"YES YES YES,
IT'S ANOTHER GREAT DAY!"

With a smile on my face
and a rainbow in my sky,
I feel light as a feather,
and I could almost fly.

With a frown on my face
made towards the rainbow,
my whole day is starting
with a big "NO, NO, NO!"

On the **YES** days my breakfast
looks scrum-diddlie-yum…

so I call out,

"I LOVE THIS FOOD!
THANKS, MY AWESOME MUM!"

I devour each mouthful,
and I lick my chops.
My tummy's feeling yummy,
and my day's looking tops.

and I scrumple my face up
as I chew, chew, chew.

I give up, spit it out,
and push my plate aside,

"I HATE YOU MUM!"

I shout out loud as I storm outside.

On the **YES** days the rain brings
a sparkle to my eye...

as I rush outside and jump
to splash things that are dry.

"ISN'T LIFE SO WONDERFUL?"
I sing and twirl around,
landing with a giggle
in a puddle on the ground.

On the **NO** days the rain
outside is looking grim,

AND I STAY OUT THERE BECAUSE
I DON'T WANNA GO BACK IN.

"You're ruining my life!"
I shout out, feeling bleak,
as the rain and my tears
roll together down my cheek.

My **YES** day afternoons
are filled with lots of surprises:
a new puzzle, blowing bubbles,
and costume disguises.

I CALL TO MY FRIEND,
"HAVING AS MUCH FUN AS ME?"
as we scramble together
up my favorite tree.

The **NO** day afternoons
are a very dull affair:
a stupid puzzle, boring bubbles,
and dressing like a bear.

"GET AWAY FROM ME!"

I call to the kid who wants to play,
as I climb up my tree alone
and hide there to sulk all day.

When the **YES** days are over
and I'm snuggled in bed...

thoughts of joy and happiness
are floating 'round my head.

I SAY, "THANKS FOR THIS DAY
AND ALL THE FUN IT'S BEEN,"

and I can't wait for what'll happen
tonight in my dream.

When the **NO** days are over
it still comes with a fight,
my pillow isn't comfy
and my blanket's not right.

I roll over crossly
and say, "it's just not fair!"

AND I BET THIS DAY WILL END
WITH A HORRIBLE NIGHTMARE!

So if I wake tomorrow and see
a **NO** day coming on,
I'll stop it in its tracks and shout,
"NO, BE GONE!"

And I'll change it to a **"YES"**
as quick as quick can be,
then I know that my day
will work out wonderfully.

Every day we have a choice
between a **YES** and a **NO**,
even if it's raining
or our games don't flow.

So when you wake up to the day,
say, "**YES, YES, YES**"
to whatever life brings you,
and your day will be the best!

DRAW YOUR WORST
NO DAY

DRAW YOUR BEST
YES DAY